DILYS PRICE

NORMAN PRICE

BELLA LASAGNE

JAMES

SARAH

MEET ALL THESE FRIENDS IN BUZZ BOOKS:

Thomas the Tank Engine

The Animals of Farthing Wood

Wind in the Willows

Winnie-the-Pooh

Fireman Sam

First published in Great Britain by Buzz Books,
an imprint of Reed Books, Children's Publishing
Michelin House, 81 Fulham Road, London SW3 6RB
and Auckland, Melbourne, Singapore and Toronto

ISBN 1 85591 323 2

Printed in Italy by Olivotto

WINDY WEATHER

Story by Rob Lee
Illustrations by The County Studio

It was a very windy day in Pontypandy. Fireman Sam looked out of the window at the trees swaying in the strong breeze.

"I'm glad we had a calm day for the Fun Run yesterday," he thought. "Station Officer Steele will be pleased with the money we raised for the Pontypandy Children's Hospital. I'll take this money with me to the fire station right now."

Sam put the money into a brown envelope and wrapped up warmly against the wind.

Sarah and James were outside Sam's house playing football.

"Hello, you two," called Sam.

As he stepped outside the door, James kicked the ball high in the air.

"Watch out, Uncle Sam!" warned Sarah.

But it was too late. The ball landed on Sam's head with a THUMP.

"Ouch!" he cried, dropping the envelope in surprise.

"Sorry, Uncle Sam," apologised James.

Fireman Sam rubbed his head. "Well, there's nothing broken. Just be more careful next time."

As he bent down to pick up the money, a gust of wind caught the envelope and blew it down the street.

"Quickly!" called Sam. "The money for the children's hospital is in that envelope!"

Sam and the twins chased after the envelope, but the wind swept it higher and higher into the sky. As they watched gloomily, the envelope flew high over Pontypandy, then disappeared from view.

"Daro!" groaned Sam in dismay. "We'll never catch it now."

Fireman Sam and the twins had been so busy chasing the envelope, they hadn't noticed Firefighter Penny Morris driving up the road in Venus, her rescue tender.

"What's up?" she asked.

Sam explained the problem. "I'd better go tell Station Officer Steele," he said, and trudged off to the station.

Penny thought for a moment, then said
brightly, "I have an idea. We'll organise our
own fundraiser to replace the money!"

"Brill!" said James.

"How about a raffle?" suggested Sarah.

"Perfect," replied Penny. "Jump in. We've
got work to do!"

11

At the fire station, Auxiliary Firefighter
Trevor Evans was in the office with Station
Officer Steele.

"With these strong winds I expect we'll
have a few call-outs today," said Station
Officer Steele.

At that moment Sam walked in.

"That's not all of our problems," said Fireman Sam. "I've lost the money that we raised for the children's hospital."

Once again, Sam told how the wind had blown the money away.

"We can't let the children down," said Station Officer Steele.

Just then a message came over the telex.

"Jump to it, crew," ordered Station Officer Steele. "The wind has blown down the weather vane at Pontypandy church! It could be dangerous!"

The firefighters dashed out of the station and onto the forecourt, where Jupiter was waiting. They climbed aboard the fire engine and raced towards Pontypandy town centre with the lights flashing and sirens blaring.

When they arrived at the church, the firefighters quickly got to work.

"The weather vane is hanging from the spire," Station Officer Steele observed. "We'll need the cutting equipment."

Trevor positioned the extension ladder against the outside of the church.

"Oh dear, the ladder isn't long enough to reach the spire," he said. "What are we going to do now?"

14

"You'll have to go in through the church window and make your way up the tower from inside," Station Officer Steele told Sam and Trevor. "There's a trap door at the top of the tower which leads to the roof."

Sam went to get the metal cutters from Jupiter's locker, while Trevor positioned the ladder beneath the church window.

"That's lucky," said Trevor. "The ladder just reaches the window."

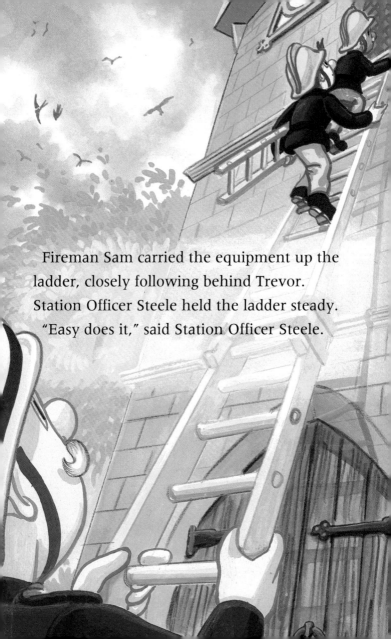

Fireman Sam carried the equipment up the ladder, closely following behind Trevor. Station Officer Steele held the ladder steady. "Easy does it," said Station Officer Steele.

Inside the tower, Fireman Sam found a ladder leading to a trap door.

"That door must lead to the roof," said Sam. "I know you don't like heights, Trevor, so I'll go up first."

"Nonsense," Trevor protested bravely. "Heights don't bother me."

Trevor stepped towards the ladder, accidentally tripping over the cutters and into the belfry!

Quickly, he reached out for the bell rope to
stop his fall. The bell bonged loudly.

"Help!" Trevor cried. "I can't stand heights!"

"Steady," called Fireman Sam, as he
grabbed Trevor and pulled him to safety.

"Th-thanks, Sam," gulped Trevor.

"Are you all right?" asked Sam.

"Except for my eardrums," he groaned.

Fireman Sam climbed the ladder and opened the trap door to the roof. Trevor reluctantly followed.

"It looks as if nobody's been up here for years," he said.

Dead leaves had piled up on the roof, and were now blowing about in the gale.

"They must have been blown up here by the gale," replied Sam.

"Can we go back down now?" called
Trevor nervously.

"We haven't got what we came for," said
Sam. "One of us will have to climb the spire
to get the weather vane."

Trevor peered over the roof. It was a long
way down.

"Don't worry," said Sam. "I'll climb up the
spire. You just hold the extra ladder steady."

Carefully, Sam climbed to the top of the spire. The wind howled around his ears.

"It's a bit blowy up here," he said, but his words got lost in the wind.

"H-hurry up, Sam," called Trevor, clinging onto the ladder below.

Fireman Sam quickly cut the weather vane away from the spire and climbed down the ladder.

"It's not a danger any more," he said, as he examined the broken vane. "But I think it's had its day."

"Can we go back inside the church tower now?" asked Trevor.

Fireman Sam grinned. "Down you go, Trev. I'll be right behind you."

As Sam watched Trevor descend the
ladder into the tower, he noticed a familiar
brown envelope amongst the piles of leaves
on the roof.

"Great fires of London!" he exclaimed,
picking it up. "This is the money I lost this
morning. The wind must have blown it all
the way up here!"

24

Station Officer Steele was waiting for Sam and Trevor when they reached the ground.

"Well done!" he said. "You've retrieved the weather vane, and you've found the Fun Run money. I say, well done!"

The firefighters at the fire station were
celebrating with a cup of tea, when Penny
and the twins arrived.

"Look, Uncle Sam!" said James excitedly.

"We've organised a raffle and raised the hundred pounds you lost," added Sarah.

"You have?" said Fireman Sam. He began to laugh. "Well done, you two. But I've already found the money from the Fun Run. It had blown onto the church tower."

"What shall we do with all the money we raised?" asked Penny.

"I know!" said Sam. "If all the ticket holders agree, we can buy a new weather vane with the proceeds of the raffle!"

"Superb idea," said Station Officer Steele.

The next day everyone gathered at Pandy Park for the raffle.

"What's the prize?" asked Trevor.

"Shh, Trevor," said Fireman Sam. "The twins are about to pick the winning ticket."

On the bandstand, Sarah scrambled up the tickets, then handed one to James.

"The winner is..." called James, "Auxiliary Firefighter Trevor Evans!"

"I've won! I've won!" shouted Trevor.

"Congratulations," said Sarah. "You've won a trip in a hot air balloon!"

"Oh no," groaned Trevor. "A hot air balloon? But I hate heights!"

FIREMAN SAM

STATION OFFICER
STEELE

TREVOR EVANS

ELVIS
CRIDLINGTON